Very little Cinderella

Teresa Heapy
&
Sue Heap

HOUGHTON MIFFLIN HARCOURT   Boston   New York

For David Fickling
and Simon Mason,
with love and thanks.
— T.H.

For Ness and Alice
with huge thanks.
—S.H.

Originally published in Great Britain by Doubleday,
a division of Random House Children's Publishers UK, 2015

www.hmhco.com

The text of this book is set in OPTI Adminster Book.
The illustrations are watercolor and ink.

ISBN 978-0-544-28223-0

Manufactured in China
TOP 10 9 8 7 6 5 4 3 2 1
4500513413

Very Little Cinderella was cleaning the house.
"I clean it all up," she said.

She cleaned the floor.

She cleaned the walls.

She cleaned the table.

Soon everything was looking very clean.

The Ugly Sisters crashed in.

"**Very** Little **Cinderella!**" they said.

"Can you please clean up?"

"No," said **Very** Little Cinderella.

"Cleaning all done."

"BUT–" said the Ugly Sisters.

"No!" said Very Little Cinderella.

"Cleaning all done.

Now I have cookie."

Cookie Tin

Suddenly, the Fairy Godmother appeared.

Who she? said Very Little Cinderella.

I'm the babysitter! said the Fairy Godmother.

"You see," said the Ugly Sisters, "we're off to a party now ..."

"I go too?" asked Very Little Cinderella.

"Er, no," said the Ugly Sisters. "Just us ..."

"But I DO go!" said Very Little Cinderella.

"We'll be back after midnight,"
said the Ugly Sisters. "Be good. Sleep tight!"

And off
they went.

Quickly.

Very Little Cinderella was very upset.

"It not fair!" she wailed.

"I not stay **here!**
I want to go **toooo!**"

The Fairy Godmother took a deep breath...

"Why don't we have a snack?" she said.
"After we clean this all up."

Then the Fairy Godmother whispered, "Listen,
why *don't* we go to the party too?

You'll need a special dress!"

"I like that!" said **Very** Little Cinderella.

"I want my **blue** dress."

"Well, it must be *special*," said the Fairy Godmother.
"What about . . .

a shiny dress

a bright dress

a tiny dress

a tight dress

a puffy-fluffy-cozy-rosy-dreamy-creamy-white dress?

A sweet dress

a curly dress

a neat dress

a frilly-silly-
crazy-daisy-
flashy-splashy-
twirly dress?

a pearly dress

Or, what about," said the
Fairy Godmother,
with one last effort ...

"a silver dress?"

"I want my blue dress,"
said Very Little Cinderella, firmly.

"And my stripey hat,

my froggy coat,

and my
lello boots!"

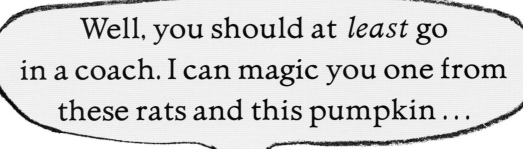

Well, you should at *least* go in a coach. I can magic you one from these rats and this pumpkin ...

said the Fairy Godmother.

Oh, NO!

said **Very** Little **Cinderella**

I go on my **BIG** blue scooter.

So they went to the party on the big blue scooter.
"We must leave at *midnight*,"
said the Fairy Godmother.

Very Little Cinderella ran into the party.
"I do dancing!" she said.

She leapt and she jumped,
she hopped and she bumped.
She swished and she swirled,
she swooshed and she twirled.

She found a friend. And another. And another.

But then . . .

...the clock struck **twelve**.

"It's midnight! Come on, time to go home!" said the Fairy Godmother.

"Nooo!**"**
said **Very** Little Cinderella.

"I stay here! I do more dancing!"

And ...

"I lost my LELLO BOOT!"

7
8
9
10 11
12

"I'll magic you some new boots," said the Fairy Godmother.

"But we have to go NOW!"

And she took
Very <small>Little</small> Cinderella
home on the
big blue scooter.

The next day, **Very** Little Cinderella was feeling very sad.

The Ugly Sisters
tried a cookie.

They tried
a balloon.

The Fairy Godmother
tried a big basket
of boots.

But nothing worked.

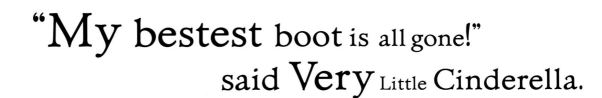

"My bestest boot is all gone!"
said Very Little Cinderella.

Just then, there was a knock at the door.

There stood a **Very** Little Prince with his mommy.

"Is this your boot?" he said. "It's a very nice boot."

My best boot!

said **Very** Little **Cinderella**.

And she gave the boot a **big** hug.

Then **Very** Little Cinderella noticed something.
"Oh," she said. "You got boots, too."

"Oh, yes, " said the **Very** Little Prince.
"I got spots all over on mine."
"Shall we have a try-on?" said **Very** Little Cinderella.

So **Very** Little Cinderella
tried on the
Very Little Prince's boot.

The **Very** Little Prince
tried on
Very Little Cinderella's boot.

It fits me!

they
said.

And **Very** Little Cinderella and the **Very** Little Prince
had a playdate.

They laughed and chased,
they wrestled and raced.

And
they both played
happily ever
after.